Ginger & Pesky

Verlyn Flieger

Illustrated by Jen Gosselin

Signum Press

ISBN (paperback): 978-1-959360-10-0
ISBN (ebook): 978-1-959360-11-7

Illustrated by Jen Gosselin

Contents

In Memory of Vaughn

Outside

When they brought her home from the shelter they called her Ginger, saying that her fur was the exact color of a ginger cookie. They gave her one to sample, but the spice prickled her tongue, so she spat it out and shot them a look that warned, *Don't try that again*. Instead they gave her kibbles, and that felt proper for a cat, so she ate them. They scratched behind her ears and brushed her fur to keep it fluffy, and that felt proper, too, and so for a while all went well.

The apartment was on the second floor, up a flight of stairs and with windows looking into the trees. They kept her inside for fear, as they told her, that if she got outside, she would get lost. Instead they allowed her to sit in the big chair by the front window and see the outside from the inside. There was a lot of outside to see. She saw the birds fly back and forth on unknown errands, saw them build their nests in the maple tree that brushed its leaves against the panes of her window. She saw the fledglings learn to fly and leave home to build nests of their own. She saw the squirrels chase each other up and down and round and round the trunk of the tree. She saw how they piled leaves for sleeping places way up where the branches forked, a perch even higher than the birds.

Sometimes the window was open, and warm air came through the screen and tickled her whiskers. Other times it was shut, and cold rain fell and ran in drops down the panes. Sometimes the green leaves on the tree turned red and yellow, and wind chased them about and danced them against the window in flurries that tapped on the glass. Sometimes white snow came soft and silent to pile up on the bare tree branches and gather on the windowsill and make the window cold where her nose pressed against it. The snow would stay for a while, and then it would go away, and presently the leaves would turn green once more. This happened so regularly that she came to expect it.

But it wasn't long before she began to want more, to smell and hear and feel for herself all the things she saw second-hand through the window, the things that belonged outside. If you want a thing strong enough and long enough and hard enough, it will happen. Ginger kept on wanting, knowing that her time would come, and so it did. One day the door was open, and no one was around. She jumped down from the chair, and before they could come she ran out and down the stairs so quickly and quietly that they never heard or saw. At the foot of the stairs there was another door, and it was open too, and she took her chance and slipped through that door as well. She found herself on a cement platform only a little larger than her chair, with railings on the sides and green shrubbery beyond the railings.

So this is Outside, she said to herself. It was bigger and colder than she expected, and not nearly as inviting at ground level as when she saw it through the window. The tree trunk rose like a tower straight and tall in front of her, and its canopy loomed over her head. The branches were so far above she could hardly see them, and the birds were just dark moving patches against the bright sky. The rough cement of the platform rasped the pads of her paws, and the harsh smell of the street stung the inside of her nose, and the shissing sound and loud honking of the cars in the roadway hurt her ears.

Just as she turned to go in she heard a click and saw that the downstairs door had swung closed behind her, shutting her out just when she was ready to go in.

She scratched with her paw, but the door did not respond. She knew of course that sooner or later they would see she was gone and come looking for her. They would pick her up and carry her inside and put her back on her chair where she belonged. So she waited patiently, but sooner turned into later, and none of that happened. Time went by, and they did not come, and the door stayed shut.

Rats! said Ginger to herself. *What am I going to do now?*

"What are you going to do now?" said a voice.

She looked up to see a squirrel sitting on a branch above her head, his tail in a double curve behind him. He was nibbling a maple seed and scattering the broken bits on her head.

"You're well and truly stuck," he told her with doleful relish. "And since you are outside," he continued, "you might as well make the most of it. Why don't you explore those bushes?"

For all her curiosity she hadn't thought of that, especially since she hadn't known the bushes were there.

Well, she said to herself, *since I'm stuck outside I might as well make the most of it. I'll just explore those bushes before I go back to my chair where it's warm and quiet.*

So she slipped down among the briars that flanked the cement stoop. Here the world was different yet again. It was dark and damp and prickly, smelling of growth and moist earth, but not nearly as nice as her chair, and even colder than the stoop. The brambles caught at her tail and tugged at her fur whenever she tried to move, so she tried not to move. That made it easy for the cold to creep under her skin and settle in her bones.

Ginger began to regret her hasty impulse. It occurred to her too late that perhaps Outside was not as good a place for a cat as she had hoped. A sudden loud sound made her jump, and the jump made the brambles scratch her even harder.

"What was that noise?" she asked the squirrel.

"A dog barking," he told her. She found out for herself soon enough when a large snout came poking through the brambles, sniffing as it came. The rest of the dog pushed into her hideout, rough and shaggy and with a pungent new smell that she didn't like at all. Without thinking, she hissed and took a swipe with her paw. The dog backed off, and Ginger pursued him through the brambles with a fierce meow and a ruffle of fur. She skidded to a halt nose to nose with the dog.

The low gravelly rumble deep in his throat was a new sound, but Ginger knew a warning when she heard one and looked frantically for a way to escape.

"Up here!" called the squirrel. She made a dash and was halfway up the trunk before his last word had died out.

"Keep coming!" urged the squirrel. "You can't stop there!"

"I can't go on either," said Ginger. "If I move, I'll fall."

She hung where she was. It was too late to back down but too scary to climb higher, so she clung suspended between sky and earth, legs extended, paws gripping and claws clutching the bark as they had never needed to grip the chair.

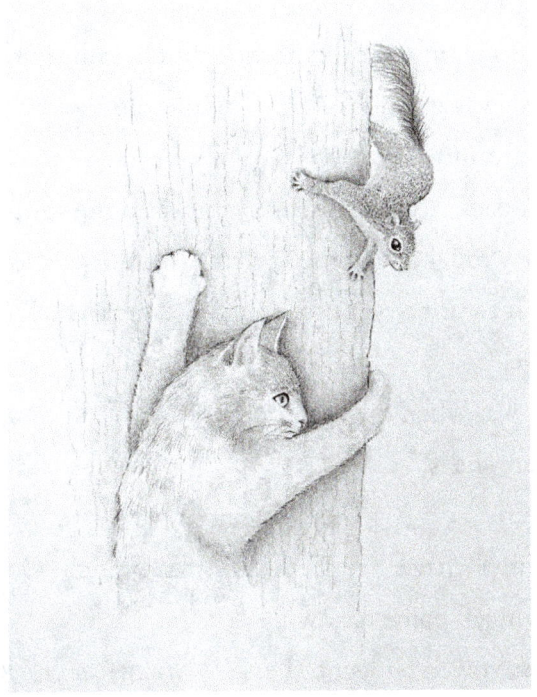

The dog was standing at full stretch on its hind legs but still unable to reach her. The heavy gusts of its breath blew against her tail like the wind that chased the leaves.

"Push and pull!" called the squirrel. "Push and pull! You can do it!"

She couldn't do it. She did it.

She pushed and pulled and jerked herself upward in convulsive bursts, each one the last until the next and then the next, and then she was up and stretched out along the branch panting with her tongue hanging out.

"Good job," said the squirrel.

For a long time she did nothing but breathe in and out, but that was enough. After a while she looked up and looked around her.

"Is outside always like this?" she asked the squirrel.

"Pretty much," said the squirrel. "You'll get used to it."

"I don't want to get used to it," she declared. "I want to go home."

That was when the door opened.

"There she is!"

"Where?"

"Up in the tree. See there? On that branch. Come on, girl. Giiinger, come daaown."

Never, vowed Ginger to herself. *I am never ever leaving this tree. Certainly not while that dog is there.*

But the dog was not there. Defeated by the tree, it had lost interest and wandered off in search of easier prey.

In the meantime, they were still standing under the tree holding their hands out, reaching up to her, but her branch was beyond their reach.

"Heeere kittykittykitty!" they coaxed. "Come. Come come comecomecome."

Ginger looked down. The ground was a long way away.

"Heeere kittykittykitty!"

I can't climb upside down, she thought. *It was hard enough when I was rightside up.*

"How do you manage?" she asked the squirrel.

"I climb upside down," said the squirrel, "and grip with my foreclaws instead of my hind ones."

"That's unnatural," said Ginger.

"It's the only way," said the squirrel.

She crept unsteadily, claws alternately gripping and slipping. At the junction of branch and tree trunk she lowered her head, stiffened her tail, and patted a tentative paw downward. And then another paw and another pat.

"Thaaat's it. Gooood kitty." More coaxing.

She was halfway when she lost her grip and went slithering and sliding headfirst and finally let go altogether, and they caught her as she fell.

They bore her back in triumph through the door and up the stairs and safely inside with all doors closed. They rewarded her with kibbles, but no one was entirely comfortable until she jumped up into her chair, turned twice around, and tucked her tail beside her paws.

"Don't try that again," they told her.

Never never never, she promised fervently, and then, *Well...maybe tomorrow...*

What's in a Name?

Ginger was dreaming in the chair by the window, her nose resting on her paws, her tail protecting both. The air was warm and summery. The breeze was soft and soothing, encouraging sleep.

And Ginger needed sleep, for she was worn out from yesterday's adventure. The memories of that were almost as exciting as the adventure itself. They replayed themselves again and again.

The first furtive dash down the stair when the chance came, the open front door and the world beyond it, things once-faraway now invading her eyes and ears and nose. And then—then the dog and the scramble up the tree to the squirrel and safety. She dreamed it over and over.

There came a tap on the window, and she woke to see two round brown eyes staring at her from the other side. It took her a minute to get them properly placed into the furry face of the squirrel.

"Hi," said the face, twitching its whiskers. "Remember me? From yesterday? I didn't mean to wake you, but I wanted to make sure you were okay. After what happened, I mean."

"Yes, I'm okay." She blinked to organize her own eyes, still fogged with sleep, and twitched her own whiskers. "Thanks for asking."

"I bet you're glad to be back home."

"Oh I don't know," said Ginger, and she stretched until her back went concave and her claws flexed like talons. "This chair is kind of boring after all that excitement."

"That was a lot of excitement," said the squirrel. "Especially the dog."

"The dog," said Ginger, and it all came rushing back, not as a dream but happening all over again.

The sudden apparition, the snuffling sound, the raw smell and snarling growl, the nose-to-nose confrontation with something she had never seen before, and then the mad scramble up the nearest tree, a slipping, sliding bundle of panic.

A shudder rippled her fur at the memory. Her stretch re-shaped itself into an arched back like a humpbacked bridge, and every hair on her body stood rigidly on end with recollection.

"I wouldn't call the dog 'boring,'" she said. "More like 'awful,' or 'horrible,' or 'unreal.' I thought for sure I was a goner that time." And she added, "I would have been if it hadn't been for you."

"Happy to help," said the squirrel. "I know that dog. He's a blowhard. All bark and no bite. His name is Ernie."

"I'll remember that," said Ginger. "By the way, what's your name?"

"It's Pesky," he said shyly. "Short for 'Pass-key.' That's what they call me in the nest, because I'm always sneaking out ahead of the others."

"Hello Pesky," said the cat. "I'm Ginger. I was named for a cookie. Pleased to meet you."

"Pleased to meet you too," said Pesky. "But if you don't mind my asking—if you were named for a cookie, shouldn't your name be Cookie? So how come is it Ginger?"

"They said it was on account of my color," said Ginger, "same as a gingersnap cookie. Anyway, Cookie is no stranger than Pass-key, if you ask me."

"I didn't ask you," said Pesky, but Ginger kept on talking. "I mean, really! 'Pass-key' sounds like an alias."

"What's an alias?" asked Pesky.

"It's a pretend name," said Ginger. "Like a nickname only for disguise, a name to hide behind. A squirrel should be called something woodsier, like 'Acorn.' Or 'Leafy.' Or 'Twig.' Something more fitting."

Pesky rose to the defense of his name. "Something more squirrely I guess you mean. By your reasoning a cat should be called 'Fluffy' or 'Purry.' Or how about 'Whiskers'? That's a cattier name than 'Ginger' if you ask me."

"I didn't ask," said Ginger, but the squirrel went right on talking.

"On the other hand," he mused, "maybe all names are strange when you look at them from the outside. Or maybe"—he warmed to his theme—"maybe everything is strange when you look at it from the outside. Maybe it all depends on your point of view."

He likes to hear himself talk, thought Ginger, *but I like to hear him talk too, so I'll keep him talking.*

"What's a point of view?" she asked.

"Just what it says it is," said Pesky. "It's the place you're looking from. It rules how you look at what you see. For example, things look different from up in a tree than they do from down on the ground."

"Or from a tree branch instead of a chair," said Ginger. She recalled how short and squat her owners had looked yesterday when she saw them from her perch on the tree branch above them.

"I think," she said, "that I'm beginning to see what you mean."

"And who knows?" said Pesky. "Maybe it's the same for names as for appearances. Maybe they only belong with certain kinds of circumstances in certain kinds of situations."

He tried to move closer and bumped his nose, which surprised him. He'd forgotten there was a window between them.

"Well, Ginger, if you ever get outside again, and if you ever feel like changing your point of view, come and see me, and I'll show you how it's done."

"I'll do that," said Ginger. "I'd like to talk more with you about point of view."

"It's a date," said Pesky. "Drop in any time."

"From a cat's point of view," said Ginger, "dropping in seems improbable. Even if I got outside, I couldn't get high enough to <u>drop</u>. I'm not a bird."

She laughed to show she was making a joke.

"But now that you've shown me how it's done, maybe I could climb, and maybe that would change my point of view."

And she did, and it did.

But that is another story.

Ginger's Great Adventure

"**P**esky, wake up."

Pesky didn't want to wake up. He was curled into a ball with his paws tucked under his chin. Warm and cozy in the squirrels' nest in the topmost branches, he was dreaming about chasing a pretty young squirrel round and round the trunk of the tree. His eyes were tight shut, but his whiskers twitched, and his legs made little running motions. "Mirabelle," he murmured.

"Pesky! Wake up!"

The voice was insistent. The words invaded his dream, but they were nothing he wanted to hear. Pesky turned over, but his eyes stayed shut. He yawned and kept right on dream-running. "Mirabelle," he murmured again.

"No. It's me. Ginger."

He opened one eye to see the cat lying on the branch just beyond his nest, stretched at full length with her paws crossed in front of her and her tail hanging down behind, looking for all the world like an illustration in a picture book.

He opened both eyes and sat up and curled his tail behind him. "Hello, Ginger!

This is a pleasant surprise! How in the world did you get here?"

"That's just what I want to tell you, but it's kind of hard to explain. It was—I had an accident."

"You mean like the other day? When the door accidentally shut with you outside?" Pesky blinked to get the sun out of his eyes and crossed his paws in front of him.

"I said *accident*," she told him, "not *accidental*. It was a mishap, something that wasn't supposed to happen. I needed to tell somebody about it, and I didn't know anybody except you, so here I am."

She needs to talk, thought Pesky.

"It happened like this. I was sitting in my chair by the window enjoying the view, but I wanted to see more. Like what you told me about point of view? All the doors were closed, so I couldn't get out. So to change my point of view I had to get from the chair onto the windowsill. But the sill was too narrow, and I bumped into the screen, and it came loose and fell out, and I fell out with it and rode it all the way down."

She licked a paw and preened her whiskers.

Wow! thought Pesky. *I bet she's never said so much at once in her whole life. I feel like I'm in the middle of a windstorm.* He felt for his own whiskers to make sure they were still attached.

He could see the scene in his mind's eye—the screen planing through the air like a hawk on an updraft and Ginger balancing in the middle like a kid on a skateboard. The picture looked both fun and funny.

"Screens aren't meant for riding on," he told her. "Us squirrels, when we want to get from place to place, we just jump. It works for us, but then, we're made for it." He uncurled his tail and climbed out to sit with her on the branch. "That sounds like a fun ride, but you're lucky you didn't get hurt."

"Cats always land on their feet," said Ginger with feline self-satisfaction. "Everybody knows that. Though I must confess I did have trouble unhooking my claws after I landed. They wouldn't untangle from the mesh."

"Never mind the mesh," said Pesky, "or your claws. What I want to know is how you got from down on the ground to up in this tree without me to tell you how to do it. Did that dog chase you? Again?"

"No," she said. "I did it all by myself. The way you taught me: *push and pull, push and pull.* Remember? You told me I could do it, and so I did it. And it was much easier than that other time, even without you there to coach me. All it takes is practice."

She gave her paws a rewarding lick.

"Way to go Ginger!" he said. "A few more tries like that and you'll be as nimble as a squirrel."

He chuckled so she would know he was making a joke.

For a minute they sat and looked at one another, face to face and nose to nose, each waiting for the other to speak.

The cat's eyes were gold and shimmery, the same color as her fur except they had a streak down the middle like a line in water. They narrowed to slits. Then they opened expectantly.

More understanding dawned on Pesky. *Ginger is lonesome! She doesn't have a friend to play with, like me and Mirabelle.*

"Well now that you're here," he said, "what are you going to do?"

"I haven't made any plans, yet," said Ginger. "Who's Mirabelle?"

"Oh," he waved a casual paw, "just someone I know. Why do you ask?"

"You said the name in your sleep. And that made me think of what we talked about the other day—you know, names and what makes them fit. How I'm named for a cookie and yours is a nickname. And what kind of name is Mirabelle? It doesn't sound to me like a squirrel name," she went on, "and that makes me wonder about names and where they come from and why, and what they mean, and...and I don't have anybody to talk about it with except you."

I was wrong, thought Pesky. *She does have a friend. It's me. Well then,* he told himself, *you'd better act like one.*

"Names are ways of knowing," he told Ginger and himself. "When we first met the other day, we were just a squirrel and a cat with a tree between us. And now we're Ginger and Pesky."

And so they were, with more adventures to share.

But those are for another story.

Ginger Drops In

It was a fine fall day, with bright sunshine and a cool breeze making the leaves of the maple tree dance over and under and all around Ginger and Pesky, who were sitting on one of the lower branches chatting comfortably face to face.

For a cat and a squirrel to meet is not usual, but the unusual was usual for Ginger and Pesky, who more and more found themselves less and less concerned about what was usual and what was not.

"Drop in any time," Pesky said, and Ginger accepted his invitation. She climbed up, and he scrambled down, and they met midway.

"You know," said Ginger, flexing her claws, "it's actually pleasant up here, once you get used to the fact that a tree branch is not a chair."

She was lying at full length along the branch. A blown leaf fluttered up against her nose, making her sneeze, and she raised a paw to brush it away.

"I like being high up," she went on, "and the fresh air and the point of view. People on the ground look short and squatty from up here. And they never look up, the sillies. There's a whole world over their heads, and they don't even know it's there."

Pesky was sitting upright with his tail curled behind him. He was holding a maple seed between his paws, nibbling the kernel and letting the bits fall through the leaves.

"I'm glad you do," Pesky said, "but I'd like to know how you got here this time around. Did you ride a screen like the other day?"

"No such luck," said Ginger. "And no such fun either. Adventures like that don't come along every day. This time

I just slipped out when somebody came to the door and then climbed the tree the way you taught me."

She smoothed her whiskers.

"They never even saw me go. It's easy once you know how. You wait till they're busy talking, and then you sneak between their feet. It's one of the tricks I learned in the Shelter."

"What's the Shelter?" asked Pesky. "Is it a Nest? Like what squirrels have?"

"Sort of, but not nearly as nice. A Shelter is a place where they put stray animals. They chase them down and lock them up.

Pesky stopped nibbling. "You can't run or jump?"

"You can't do either. Specially not when the place full of other cats all wanting to get out just like you. You're well and truly stuck."

"So how did you get well and truly unstuck? Because, here you are."

"The Shelter gives away its animals to people who want pets. Mostly cats and dogs. My owners, the people I live with now, wanted a cat. So they came to the Shelter, and they saw me and took me away. And here I am."

"What happened between *there* and *here*?"

"A lot. No sooner was I out of the cage than I was stuffed into another, smaller cage where I couldn't stand up or turn around, and my nose was pushed right up against the wire."

She sneezed again.

"When my new owners finally let me out in the place where they live, it was into a whole new space. Like a new point of view, you know?"

"Must have been odd," said Pesky.

"Very odd. Full of all kinds of strange rooms. It was immense after the cage. And so empty, with no other cats. I missed them, and most of all I missed Nubbin."

Pesky dribbled more crumbs. "Who's Nubbin?"

"Nubbin was my little brother," said Ginger.

"I didn't know you had a brother," said Pesky.

"I don't anymore," she said. "I'll never see him again."

She stopped talking for a moment, then went on.

"Nubbin was the runt of the litter, smaller than the others, so I sort of took care of him. We'd curl around each other to keep warm when we slept and talk to each other and play games and chase each other around."

Like me and Mirabelle, thought Pesky.

"We lived in a battered old trash can somebody left in an alley. I guess that's kind of like a Nest. And then one day people came and picked us out of the trash can and took us to the Shelter. It was in the Shelter that Nubbin lost his tail."

"What do you mean, 'lost it?' How can you lose your own tail? Your tail is part of you."

"I don't mean he misplaced it. It got caught in the cage door, and when he tried to pull it loose, it broke, so they cut it off. They bandaged the stump, and it finally healed, but he still looked funny without a tail. That's why they called him Nubbin and why nobody wanted him. For all I know he's still in the cage waiting for someone to find him."

Pesky couldn't make up his mind whether to feel sad or angry and decided to go for both.

"I hope somebody nice and kind has found him by now and taken him out of the cage. Didn't you find it demeaning and demoralizing to be handed around like that? Like a parcel?" he asked. "I certainly would have."

"Neither demeaning or demoralizing," she told him. "Just boring. It makes me thankful that I have someone intelligent to talk to. Like you."

"Or like Nubbin," said Pesky, and no sooner had he uttered the words than he wanted to unsay them. But by then it was too late. It always is.

"Or like Nubbin," said Ginger.

The shadow that fell across her face as she spoke was the shadow of a leaf falling, but to Pesky's eyes it came from inside, swallowing Ginger's light and turning it dark and full of sorrow.

After that there seemed little more to say, and face to face and eye to eye on the tree branch Ginger and Pesky fell silent, both together and each with separate thoughts, while around them the leaves danced their autumn dance and blew in the wind.

Pesky and Ginger and Nubbin and Mirabelle

Nubbin the cat and Mirabelle the squirrel were only memories, bright shadows that crisscrossed one another in the minds of their imaginators, Pesky the squirrel and Ginger the cat.

But what if memories have minds of their own?

Pesky knew that Ginger mourned the loss of her brother, Nubbin, the cat who lost his tail. So he could imagine Nubbin, tailless and forlorn, calling to Ginger from the back of the cage in the Shelter, "Ginger! Don't go! Don't leave me!" He could also imagine Ginger answering as she was carried away, "Nubbin! I don't want to go! I didn't mean to leave you!"

But Pesky knew that it was already too late. Ginger was gone: adopted and taken away by her new owners. She and Nubbin would never see each other again.

Ginger knew that Pesky had only to close his eyes to see Mirabelle, the squirrel he chased through his dreams, whose name he murmured in his sleep. Ginger could imagine Mirabelle always just ahead of Pesky, always calling, "Catch me if you can!" as they chased each other round and round and up and down the trunk and branches of the tree.

"At least," she might think, "chasing Mirabelle keeps Pesky alert. A bored squirrel is a dull squirrel, and a dull squirrel is a boring squirrel."

Imagine if Ginger's and Pesky's memories could open their doors to one another, what Ginger's memory of Nubbin might say to Pesky's memory of Mirabelle?

What a story that would be!

But who will write it?

Arboreal

Interruption

Pesky and Ginger, the squirrel and the pussycat, were sitting and chatting on their favorite branch of their favorite tree. It was their favorite time of the afternoon when the late sun, its rays almost horizontal, cast its light over their world and turned everything in it to gold, including them.

"Excuse me," said a voice, breaking in on their conversation. The voice was soft and whispery, like the rustle of green leaves in a summer breeze.

"What?" said Pesky.

"I said, 'excuse me,'" said the voice.

"I'm not offended," said Pesky and then blinked in surprise as he added, "Hey wait a minute!" followed by "Who are you?" followed by "Where are you?" as he looked around to locate the speaker.

But there was no one.

"Who are you talking to?" asked Ginger.

"Didn't you hear a voice?"

"I thought that was just leaves rustling," she told him. "I didn't see anybody else around."

"Neither did I," said Pesky. "That's just the problem. There isn't anybody else around, just the two of us. But somebody said 'excuse me' just now."

"Excuse me," said the voice again, with a trace of melancholy, "but you couldn't be more wrong. There is somebody else around. It's me. I am around. In fact, I've been around all along. In fact, I am always around. It's you and your cat friend who come and go."

"Not," she added, "that I object to coming and going. No, no, not at all! It's a refreshing change from standing still, which is what I do all day. I said 'excuse me' to be polite, because I was interrupting you, and I was interrupting you because I wanted to join your conversation."

"You've done more than join it," said Ginger. "You've stopped it in its tracks. But it might revive," she added hopefully, "if we could see you. How come you're invisible?"

"I'm not invisible," said the voice. "I'm just too big to be seen."

Ginger looked up, looked down, looked all around. "You're right about that," she said. "Okay, I give up. Where are you, and why can't we see you?"

"You can't see me because you don't know how to look," said the voice with a touch of severity. "But as a matter of fact you should see me, because I'm right here where I've been all along. I am the tree you climbed, Ginger, to get away from that dog the other day. I am the tree you visit when you want to chat with your friend Pesky. I am the tree where you nest at night, Pesky, in a pile of leaves high up in my branches. I am the tree whose seeds you nibble when you're hungry. I am the tree where you chase and play games with your friend Mirabelle. I am the silver maple tree you're sitting on right now. My name is Silvie. How do you do?"

"How do you do?" said Pesky.

"Pleased to meet you," said Ginger. "Um, I hope you don't mind being sat on."

"Not in the least," said Silvie. "I am happy to have company."

"We mean no disrespect," added Pesky, "but there aren't many places where a squirrel and a cat can meet, and you are a convenient place."

"My pleasure," said Silvie. "In the natural course of things I should have been in a forest with other trees all around for company. But on a city street," she sighed and her leaves rustled, "there are no other trees close enough to talk with. I can signal, of course, the way trees signal to other trees with their branches, and it's a good way of communicating over distance. But a real conversation like the one the two of you were having—that is not what trees have been accustomed to. In fact, this is my first conversation. Ever. I am enjoying it very much."

She sure talks a lot, thought Ginger. *But then, she has no friends to talk to. Like me before I met Pesky.*

Silvie is lonely, thought Pesky. *Like Ginger when I first met her. That's why she's talking so much.*

"I'm glad you're having a good time now," said Pesky.

"You're welcome to join our conversation any time you feel like it," said Ginger.

"Thank you," said Silvie. "I'll do that."

The Cat's Meow

"I don't mind being called a house cat," said Ginger, stretching her backbone, elevating her hinder parts, and raising her tail above them like a flagpole, "but I draw the line at being called a pet."

It was the midday lull—lunch hour to humans—and the cat and the squirrel were chatting comfortably on their favorite tree-limb, a branch that stuck out at a right angle from the trunk and offered a convenient place to sit and gossip.

"What's wrong with being called a pet?" asked Pesky. He was grooming his tail, brushing the fur and fluffing it to air out. "And what is a pet anyway?"

"A pet is an animal that you keep for your amusement," she told him. "Like a toy, only real."

"I can't imagine 'keeping' an animal for any reason," said Pesky distastefully, "especially amusement. It would be like stockpiling acorns with fur. And feelings. It sounds barbaric."

"My point exactly," said Ginger with a delicate shudder.

"Who calls you a pet?" asked Pesky while giving his left ear a brisk scratching.

"My owners call me a pet," said Ginger, scratching her own ear in companionship. "It's not their fault that they don't know any better. They've been badly brought up, poor things, so I don't blame them. But someone should inform them that nobody owns a cat."

"Mind you," she added, "I'd be the first to admit that being a pet has its advantages—food and shelter and kind owners who brush your fur and scratch you behind your ears. That's not too bad."

She rearranged her paws on the tree branch, curling them to provide a cushion for her chin.

"Not if that's all it amounts to," said Pesky, twitching his tail. He was imagining acorns with fur.

"But when you look at them closely," said Ginger, "all those advantages add up to dependence, not improvement. Sometimes," she went on, "when I'm bored and restless, I try to imagine what it would be like to be a wild animal. Not completely wild, you understand—I don't mean living in the woods and having to hunt for my dinner every day— I mean just being by myself and living on my own. Kind of like you, Pesky."

"Should I take that as a compliment?" asked Pesky. But his irony escaped her.

"I mean," she said, "you're a squirrel, which is a sort of civilized wild animal."

"Two compliments in one day. You're getting soft, Ginger."

"And you're teasing me. But I think you know what I mean," she said.

"You're used to traffic and sidewalks and people passing, but at the same time, you're beholden to no one. You come and go wherever you want whenever you want; you get your own food whenever you're hungry."

"Of course," said Pesky. "That's the life of a squirrel."

"Yes, but it's not the life of a house cat, and that's my point. I get fed twice a day. That's nice, I grant you. But it's just my luck, not my choice, that the feeding times and my hungry times happen together."

"I've heard of worse things," said Pesky.

"I know, it makes me sound spoiled and pettish, excuse the pun. But really, owners expect too much from their pets. They expect animals to understand them, but they don't try to understand animals. They pretend to, but they don't, not really."

"I think you're asking for too much," said Pesky. "Everyone knows how stupid they are."

"On the contrary, they're actually quite intelligent," said Ginger, "in their own way. They just need time to work things out."

"Too much time for me," said Pesky.

"Like the time I upset my water bowl," said Ginger, "and all the water ran out on the floor, and my paws got wet. Not having fingers, I couldn't turn the bowl right side up, so I had to get my owner to come and pick it up and mop up the spill. I tried and tried to tell her, but no matter how loud I meowed, she couldn't understand a word I was saying, just kept meowing back at me every time I spoke up. As if we were having a conversation but she didn't know the words."

"I can see how that would be frustrating," said Pesky.

"I finally screeched so loud it must have hurt her ears."

"RREEAAOOOWWWRRR!"

**"By which I meant to say, '*I have upset my water bowl!!
Quit talking nonsense and come and clean it up, you stupid
nit! My paws are all wet and drippy!*'**

"Well, she may be stupid, but she's not dumb. That got
her attention. She came trotting after me, and I showed
her where the water was spilled. Once she saw the problem,
she knew just what to do, mopped up the spill, and refilled
the bowl with clean water. And to her credit she did
say, 'Thank you, Ginger, for telling me about this.' But
the whole episode took me half a morning from spill to
cleanup. She was holding a book at the time; that's what
made her so slow."

"What's a book?" asked Pesky.

Ginger narrowed her eyes and curled her tail. "I can tell
you <u>what</u> it is," she said, "but I can't explain <u>why</u>."

She took a deep breath and began.

"A book," she said slowly, careful to get it right, "is a box
with sides that open out and a stack of papers inside. The
papers are all marked over and scratched up. People hold
the book open on their laps and stare at the inside paper.
Then they turn it over and look at the other side. And so
on and so on until they get to the end."

None of it made sense to Pesky.

"Paper?" he asked. "You mean the stuff that folds around food? The stuff people drop on the sidewalk? Why would anyone put that in a box, much less take it out and look at it?"

"Beats me," said Ginger. "Goodness knows why. I'm just telling you what I've seen."

She shook her head.

"I tried some once. I pulled a book off the bottom shelf, and it landed open with the paper falling out, so I took a bite, but after the first nibble I spit it out. It tasted terrible—dry and bitter—and the pieces stuck in my teeth. I couldn't see why my owner liked it so much. Just goes to show you what odd things people do for amusement. Like keeping pets."

"I tasted a piece of paper myself once," Pesky confided. "I saw some kid on the street unwrap a tidbit and throw away the wrapping with a piece stuck to it, so I picked it up to taste. Yuck! I was really nasty—gooey and sticky—and it made my tongue sting."

He twitched his mouth in recollection. "Never again. Once bit, twice wise, as my old dad used to say."

"You remember your dad?" asked Ginger. "I never had a dad that I can recall. Only the trashcan I grew up in, and that never gave me any advice."

"You seem to have done okay without it," said Pesky.

A Meeting of Minds

Nubbin lay curled asleep in a corner of the cage in the lost-animal shelter.

"I'm sorry to disturb you," said a squeaky voice in his ear. "But you're lying on my tail."

Nubbin jerked awake at the words. "Ginger?!" He stared wide-eyed around him, but there was nothing to see save a skinny brown rat with pink ears who was sitting half-concealed in the shadows. The rat cocked his head on one side and looked at Nubbin expectantly.

"Who's Ginger?" he asked.

"My mistake," mumbled Nubbin. "I thought you were my sister."

"'Fraid not," said the rat, carefully pulling his tail out from under Nubbin's stomach. "Not only am I not your sister, I'm not a cat at all. As one good look should tell you. I'm a rat, a different species altogether. My name is Ratkin. How do you do?"

"I'm Nubbin," said Nubbin. "Pleased to meet you, though a cat shelter seems an odd place to find a rat. Aren't you afraid I'll eat you?" He laughed to show it was a joke.

"Not with all this free food they give you people," said Ratkin. "I'm here for some of that myself. Besides, I like a spice of danger to season my dinner. Life on the edge. No risk, no reward. No pain, no gain. The game must be worth the candle. What happened to your tail?"

Nubbin sighed. The usual question. "Someone slammed the gate on it one day at feeding time, and it got broken. They had to cut it off."

"Don't you miss it?" asked Ratkin.

"Hardly at all anymore," said Nubbin. "I'm used to being tailless. And I can usually tell the difference between a cat and a rat," he went on, "only I was dreaming."

"I hope it was a pleasant dream," said the rat.

"Like I said, I was dreaming about my sister. We were playing, Ginger and me. Like in the trash can when we were kittens. I hate waking up and her not being here."

"Gone but not forgotten," said Ratkin. "When did she die?"

"She's not dead," said Nubbin, "as far as I know. People came and got her and took her away." He paused, remembering, then went on. "Someday," he said, "someday I'll go and find her."

"Good for you," said Ratkin. "Stick by your kin. How will you know where to look for her?"

"The folks who took her away, I heard them say where they lived. A street with numbers. I know about streets from living in the trash can. We mostly stayed in the alley, but there were streets all around."

My young friend, thought Ratkin, *you are a brave but foolhardy cat, and you don't know what you're getting into.*

You are appallingly innocent and naïve, and you need taking care of in the worst way. I'll have to look after you, or you'll run into trouble just as soon as you get started.

He sighed. "When were you thinking of going?"

"I dunno exactly," said Nubbin. "Sometime soon."

"Any particular time?"

"After feeding time, I guess."

"Good planning" said the rat. "There's always commotion then, and no one will notice one cat missing among the many. Evening feeding would be best. Most visitors will have left, and they'll be starting to close the place up for the night. So tonight at feeding time follow me, and do just what I do."

This was too fast for Nubbin. "You mean right away?" he said. "Tonight?"

"Yes of course tonight. No time like the present. Seize the moment. He who hesitates is lost."

"Do you have to say so many things all at once?" said Nubbin. "You're making my head spin."

"Just messing about in quotes," said Ratkin. "What I mean to say is stick close behind me, and I'll guide you."

"Okay," said Nubbin.

"Now I advise you to go back to sleep," said Ratkin. "You need to conserve your strength."

Obediently, Nubbin lay down and put his chin on his paws. The last thing he saw before he closed his eyes was Ratkin, who crept close and whispered in his ear. "Until tonight," he said, and in the blink of an eye, he had melted into the shadows and was gone.

"Ginger," murmured Nubbin and fell fast asleep.

Thus it was that the plan was formed; the bargain was made; the die was cast.

Evening came and with it pandemonium as the iron gate swung open and cats scrambled yowling over and around each other to be first at the feeding bowls. Nubbin was an old hand at this and had woken up, found a full bowl, and demolished its contents before Ratkin found him in the crowd.

"Ready?" he asked.

"Just cleaning my whiskers," said Nubbin. "Yes, I'm ready."

"Then here we go." Ratkin crept low on his belly to the left side of the cage where the gate latched. Nubbin followed him, trying as much as he could to look like a rat.

"Lie flat," hissed Ratkin. "Melt into the background." Nubbin followed orders. Gradually the uproar died as bowls were emptied and cats retired to groom their whiskers and clean their paws. The gate opened, and the bowls started stacking up just outside.

"Now!" hissed Ratkin.

He slid past the stack of bowls. Nubbin followed. He looked like a cat trying to look like a rat, but nobody was paying attention, and he heard to his surprise a loud metallic clang as the gate latched shut with him on the other side. The outside.

He took a deep breath.

"Comeon-comeon-comeon!" squeaked Ratkin. "No time to dally!"

Fitting themselves into the angled space where the floor met the wall, the two animals scuttled on their bellies, trying to look like pieces of stone, concrete, flagstone flooring, anything but what they actually were—two living creatures running for dear life away from prison, from captivity, from the world of the caught and captured, running headlong into freedom, into the danger that was waiting for them on all sides.

Out the automatic door just as it locked into place, dodging the feet that kept stomping down around their ears, skittering off the sidewalk down into the gutter for shelter until "Stop!" called Nubbin. "I'm out of breath! I can't run anymore!"

"In here!" cried Ratkin ducking under a curb drain, and Nubbin followed him into the dark, damp hollow where they lay panting, looking out at rush hour traffic with wary eyes like frightened visitors from another world, which was, if you stop to think about it, exactly what they were.

***

The rest of their journey was a repetition with variations of that first heart-pounding escape, a reiteration many times relived, remembered and restaged. Even the scenery, after that first breakout from the shelter, was the same backdrop endlessly repeated. City streets, rushing traffic, pounding feet, corners where everyone stopped and waited, then in clumps went on again. Lights flashed red and green; horns blared and echoed off the stony surfaces of civilization while overhead the green world waited to reclaim its birthright and recover the surface of the earth.

At last they arrived, footsore and draggled, at the foot of a tree on the right street at the right house number.

"How will we know if she's here?" asked Nubbin.

"We'll inquire," said Ratkin.

And they did.

And she was.

Nubbin and His Friend

It was the middle of the night, and Pesky the squirrel was deep asleep in his nest high up in the tree-branches when he was awakened by the sound of voices in the street below.

"Are you sure this is the place?" said one voice. If a meow could be anxious, this one was.

The other voice was smooth and reassuring. "Looks like it to me," it said and added, "It fits the description we got at the Shelter."

The voice was attached to a large, brown rat with pink ears and a long tail.

"But how will we know if she's here?" said the anxious voice.

"We'll inquire."

Pesky opened one bleary eye and peered over the edge of the nest. "Hello down there! Are you looking for someone?"

"Yes," said a shadowy figure. "My sister. I heard tell she lives around here somewhere."

"Who are you?"

"I'm Nubbin," said the voice.

Nubbin! thought Pesky. *Ginger's brother. The cat without a tail. How in the world did he get here?*

"Is your sister a cat named Ginger?" he asked the shadowy figure.

"That's her!" said Nubbin. "Please," he said eagerly, "will you tell her I'm here?"

The smooth voice interrupted. "Nubbin, mind your manners." Then to Pesky with careful courtesy, "How do you do? My name is Ratkin."

"Nice to meet you, Ratkin," said Pesky.

"You'll have to excuse my young friend," the rat went on. "He grew up in a cage, so he's not used to meeting strangers. Nubbin, say 'How do you do?'"

"Hiya!" said Nubbin. He was a ginger-colored cat with a stub where his tail should have been.

"Hello, Nubbin," said Pesky. "I've heard a lot about you."

The courtesies over, he got down to business. "Ginger doesn't live in this tree. She lives in that house over there. The one with the steps leading up to the front door. But she's probably asleep," he added, yawning. "Most of us are at this time of night."

"Are you a friend of Ginger's?" asked Nubbin.

"I guess you could say that," he told the shadow. "But I'm a little short of sleep right now, so if you'll excuse me, I'm going back to bed."

He pulled in his head and burrowed deep into the leaves of the nest hoping the shadowy figures would take his not-so-subtle hint and go away. They didn't. They settled down at the foot of the tree and seemed prepared to spend the night. So was he.

The next morning the sun was shining. There was not a cloud in the sky; the air was cool and clear; and the breeze was gentle. Pesky, too, was in better temper. He scrambled down the tree to where two shapes lay near the base of the trunk. Both were sound asleep.

"Good morning," said Pesky. The pink-eared shape opened his eyes and stood up when he saw Pesky. "Good morning," he said. "Are you the person who spoke to us last night?"

"That was me. And you'd better wake your friend if he's hoping to see Ginger. They usually let her out around mid-morning."

The ginger-colored shape turned over and put his paws over his ears.

"Who's They?" asked Ratkin. "Her owners?"

"So they suppose." Pesky chuckled. "Ginger says no one owns a cat. They may think they do, but the cat knows better."

It was then that the door opened and a fluffy, golden cat with brown rings around her tail stuck her nose out the door.

At the sight of her, Pesky swung into action.

"Ginger!" he called to her. "Ginger! Look who's here!" Then, "Wake up!" he chittered at Nubbin. "Wake up sleepyhead! There she is! There's your sister."

At the sight of Nubbin, Ginger's eyes widened to circles, then narrowed to slits. She stood quite still for a moment; then slowly, cautiously, never taking her eyes off him, she padded down the steps one stealthy paw at a time, as if she were stalking prey. The tip of her tail was twitching slowly back and forth, back and forth.

On the bottom step she stopped dead, and her tail stopped twitching and stood straight up like a flagpole.

Then she gathered her muscles and pounced on the sleeping Nubbin like a cat on a mouse.

He woke up enough to wrap all four paws around her, and she wrapped her paws around him, and they rolled over and over and over one another like two kittens playing.

Then they both stopped and pulled away and each looked at the other with an equal expression of delight and disbelief.

"Ginger?" said Nubbin. "Is it really you? It's been so long since I've seen you, I almost forgot what you looked like!"

"Yes, it's really me. But is it really you Nubbin? I thought I would never see you again. How did you know where to find me? And how did you get here? It's a long way from the Shelter."

She was a fountain bubbling with questions, and Nubbin was so eager to tell about all that had happened to him that his story tumbled over itself like a waterfall in its rush to be heard.

"When those people came and took you away that day, I heard them say where they lived, and I told my friend Ratkin who used to steal food from the cage, and he said he could show me how to get there, but we would have to travel a long way mostly at night—many nights—and dodge dogs and motor cars and traffic lights and hide in dumpsters and all kinds of things. So that's what we did." He stopped for breath.

"That's quite an adventure," said Pesky. "*The Tale of the Tailless Cat.* As good as the stories my old dad used to tell. I'll save it up and tell it my own kits some day. You should be proud, Nubbin."

"I was scared," said Nubbin.

"You were brave," said Ginger. "I'm proud of you!" And she gave Nubbin a lick with her tongue.

She bumped her head against Ratkin to show her thanks. "And I'm thankful to Ratkin for guiding you so safely."

Squirrels do not cry, but Pesky's eyes grew bigger and rounder, and his nose quivered, and his whiskers twitched as he watched the coming together of Nubbin and Ginger in spite of all the odds that had been stacked against them.

"I don't want to disrupt such a fond family reunion," said Ratkin to Pesky in a quiet voice, "but I need to pee. Is there somewhere...?"

"Right over there," said Pesky, with a nod of his head. "In those bushes beside the front steps."

Just then the door of the house opened, and a voice called "Giiinger. Heeere kitty kitty kitty."

Then it stopped.

Then it said, "Hey, that's not Ginger. Or is it? Where's her tail? Kitty kitty kitty?"

"Follow me!" said Ginger to Nubbin. And in they went, the two of them together.

The Tale of the Tail

"Speaking of names..." said Pesky.

They were not, at that particular moment, speaking of names, but such details never bothered Pesky, who had a funny way of finishing out loud a thought that had started in his head. This often led to the confusion of his hearers, who were forced to think twice as fast just to keep up, never mind to get ahead.

"...who named you Nubbin, Nubbin?"

"Ginger did," said Nubbin, who was always a little confused anyway and so found Pesky's speech patterns normal, "to console me for losing my tail. She said I deserved a treat for being brave, but she had nothing else to give me, so she gave me a new name."

"It's a good name," said Pesky.

"Much obliged," murmured Ginger, who was stretched out on the bottom step of the house across the sidewalk from the tree. The others were sitting at the base of the tree, enjoying the weather and one another's company.

"...a fine name, but it doesn't seem to me to be very catlike. I'd have thought a name like "Fluffy" or "Mittens" or "Nibbles" would have been more suitable."

Ratkin sighed, and his eyelids drooped as if to block out this vision.

"What was your name before it was 'Nubbin'? he asked. "Or did you have one?"

"Oh, we all had names," said Nubbin. "The people at the Shelter gave us names so they could tell us one from another at feeding time."

"And what was yours?" said Ratkin.

"Fred," said Nubbin.

It dropped into the conversation with a dull thud, like a stone hitting dirt.

"Fred," repeated Ratkin, and after a moment's consideration, "Oh no, nonono. That doesn't fit you at all. Nubbin is a much more suitable name for the cat I see before me—a cat with a nub for a tail—besides being, as I suspect, a name with some history behind it. A story, so to speak."

"Come to think of it," he went on, "that would be a story we haven't heard yet. And a tale as much worth telling, I suspect, as the ones Pesky was regaling us with the other day. Come on, Nubbin. It's your turn to tell a story."

"You won't laugh?" said Nubbin.

"I won't let them," promised Ginger.

So he began.

"Well. I was just sitting in the cage waiting for feeding time," but right away Pesky interrupted. "What's a cage?' he asked, and Nubbin had to stop and explain.

"It's a big box but with bars instead of sides so you can see out but there's nothing outside to see except more cages with animals in them."

Pesky looked interested, so he went on. "One cage holds big dogs that bark, and one holds little dogs that yip. Sometimes they bark and yip at the same time, talking to each other."

"Sounds pretty noisy," said Pesky.

"That's putting it mildly," said Nubbin. "So noisy you can't even hear yourself think."

He shook his head, remembering.

"Go on! Go on!" urged Pesky. "This is getting good!"

"Well, there I was in the cage sitting in a corner waiting for feeding-time. I was always hungry back then because being the runt of the litter I usually got pushed aside in the general stampede, so this time I tried to get ahead of the crowd, but no luck. I got bowled over and tumbled about and about like a ball and wound up upside down right at the open gate tail first and head last."

"When they slammed the gate shut and I heard it latch, I was still inside, but my tail had wandered outside like it didn't belong to me, which alas was soon to be the case, and at first I just felt the slam like being hit with a stick, but the gate stayed shut, and before long I felt it begin to pinch and then to hurt and then to really hurt and then to really really really hurt, and I tried to pull it free, and that made it hurt even worse, so there I hung tail up and head down until they came back for the feeding bowls, and they opened the gate, and I fell to the floor, but fortunately I fell inside the cage, and Ginger came and tried to lick the hurt place on my tail, but that made it hurt even worse, so she had to stop."

"I had to stop," said Ginger, "he was yowling so loud the whole Shelter echoed."

Nubbin nodded, pleased to take credit where it was due.

"What happened then?" asked Pesky.

"Oh then," said Ginger, "somebody in a blue shirt came and took Nubbin away. He was gone until the next day, and when they brought him back, he was asleep, and his tail was gone and his hind end was all bandaged up, and even when he woke up he couldn't walk for the first couple of days."

"I don't remember anything," said Nubbin, "from when I fell until when I woke up back in the cage. I didn't know what had happened to me. At first when I tried to walk I kept losing my balance and falling over and I couldn't figure out why. A tail is a useful thing. You don't realize that until you've lost it. I wish I still had mine."

"What became of it?" asked Pesky. "I mean, a tail is a real thing, even if it's cut off. They must have put it someplace."

Nubbin looked puzzled. "I never thought to ask," he admitted.

"Well, well, well," said Ratkin. "That is a story and a half and no mistake! I was captured, enraptured, enthralled. You are a natural born story-teller, Nubbin. You have a gift for gab."

Nubbin ducked his head. "Thanks," he said. "I just said what happened. But that's my story, and I'm stuck with it."

"And unstuck from your tail," added Ginger.

"I don't mind," said Nubbin. "Much. I can still walk and talk and eat. And play. And I like telling stories. It makes me feel important."

"You are important," Pesky assured him. "If you hadn't come to find Ginger that night, none of us would be here today. No story would be told. Just you remember that."

"I will," said Nubbin.

And he did.

But that is another story.

Tale Telling

S ome were able to climb the tree but others could not, and so it became the custom when the four friends met—as they did most evenings in good weather—that they all gathered in and around the hollow between the two big roots at the base of the tree.

True, they didn't all fit equally.

Ratkin and Pesky found it roomy enough and indeed overlarge for a rat and a squirrel, but the two cats, Ginger and Nubbin, even curled as tight as they could wind themselves, filled the hollow to capacity and then some.

So Ginger chose instead the front step of her house across from the tree while Nubbin had a tendency to stretch his full length across the sidewalk and wait for some passer-by to step on him. Not that anyone ever did. Even without a tail he was too big for that.

The half-dark of the street lamp down the block created atmosphere, making it difficult for them all to see one another yet for that very reason giving their get-together the intimate feeling of a private party, flavoring all they said with the special quality of overheard conversation that gave ordinary words the aura of magic. This was especially true in the case of their usual audience, the tree, Silvie, who wasn't much of a talker but enjoyed listening in. Here is what she overheard one evening in late summer when the weather was just on the turn and the days were closing in:

"If my old dad could only see me now," said Pesky, sitting on his hind legs with his tail curled for balance. "He'd think I was somebody in a story. Nothing but a tall tale."

"What is a tall tail?" asked Nubbin. "A tail that's taller than its owner? I'd like to have a tall tail. I'd like to have a tail at all, tall or otherwise."

He sounded wistful, and Ginger butted her head against his for sympathy.

"Not tail like attachment," Pesky explained. "Tale like story. A tall tale is a blown-up story, one that couldn't be true, that's unbelievable, and that's why it's fun. That's how my old dad would feel if he could see me sitting here hobnobbing with cats and rats. Not," added Pesky hastily, "that he'd let himself be impressed, not that old rascal. He was a storyteller himself, in his day and a good one too, and that's why he wouldn't believe this one."

He sighed. "I wish I could remember some of the stories he used to tell us kits in the nest at night—all about squirrels getting carried off by giant birds or captured by dogs and made to dig for bones. There's an old squirrel legend that says squirrels are descended from acorns. That we were once the same species but got separated somewhere along the line. Some of us climbed down to the ground, and others stayed up in the trees. And there was another one, I remember, that went the other way, about an acorn that wanted to be a squirrel."

"Tell us that one," said Nubbin.

Pesky took a deep breath and shifted into storytelling mode. His tail fluffed to twice its size and seemed to grow bigger and curvier with each new word that he uttered.

"There was once an acorn," he said, "that wanted to be a squirrel. In spite of its size, in spite of its lack of paws or tail, much less of a mouth that could chatter, nothing would make that acorn happy but to be a squirrel.

"So he went to the Great Acorn and asked that he be turned into a squirrel.

"'Are you sure?' the Great Acorn asked him. 'Are you very sure? Because once you're changed, you're changed. I won't be able to change you back again.'

"'I'm very sure,' said the foolish acorn.

"So the Great Acorn took his thinking cap—you know, of course that all acorns have caps, but this was the biggest and the thinkingest of them all—and he thought and he thought and he thought, and all the while he was thinking the acorn was feeling itself growing and sprouting.

"First he felt two eyes pop open and blink in the sunlight.

"And then a mouth split his nice smooth hull and sprouted whiskers around it.

"And the whiskers began to twitch.

"And when he looked down at himself with his new eyes, he saw four legs sticking out at the corners, with paws on the ends of them and claws on the ends of the paws.

"And the legs began to move and bend so he could sit upright, and his front paws curled like hands that could grasp and hold.

"And at last and finally for an extra he felt a furry tail begin to curl at the end of his spine.

"It was only then that it dawned on him that he was not an acorn any longer. He was in very truth a squirrel.

"*What now?* he said to himself. *When you get what you ask for, what do you do with it?*"

"That's a good question," said Ginger from the front steps. "Why didn't he try out some squirrel behavior? Like climbing a tree. Or chasing another squirrel."

"In fact," said Pesky, "he did all of those things. Would you believe, Ginger, that I am that very acorn?"

He closed one eye in a wink, whisked his tail from side to side, and gave her a look so full of mischief that she couldn't help but laugh. It came out "meowww" but with a chuckle in it.

"Remember when we first met?" Pesky said to her, "and we were talking about names? 'Leafy' and 'Twig' and 'Purry' and 'Fluffy' and such? You suggested that 'Acorn' would be a good name for me, and you didn't even know how right you were."

He laughed a chattery, squirrelly laugh.

"Wait a minute. Wait a minute." Here came the precise, pedantic voice of Ratkin. "Are you trying to tell us, Pesky, that you are indeed and in fact an acorn and not a squirrel? I find that difficult to believe."

"I..."

Pesky opened his mouth to explain the joke, but Ratkin was ahead of him.

"Or are you saying you are a squirrel who thinks he's an acorn?"

"No, it's just a tall..."

"Or are you an acorn <u>and</u> a squirrel? Two for the price of one? A bargain!"

Ratkin was on a roll, and however hard he tried, Pesky couldn't get a word in edgewise.

"Or are you saying be satisfied with what you actually are right this minute?"

"Well, yes," said Pesky. "That's all you ever have, really. That's all anyone ever has. That should be enough."

"It's certainly enough for me," said Ginger with a cavernous yawn. "And enough for tonight, I think. It's time we were all in bed."

And it was.

As the conversation died, and the animals snuggled down in their various nooks and corners, Silvie the tree

reflected on how much you can learn by keeping your
mouth shut.

Straight Talk

"At least," Pesky continued, "that's what my old dad used to say."

He gave his ear a vigorous scratching with his left hind paw. This conclusion to what for him had been a pretty long speech just about emptied his store of words, so he said nothing further.

On this warm, sunny afternoon the animals were enjoying the weather in their favorite spots.

Pesky was perched squirrel-fashion on his branch of the tree across the way, giving him a squirrel's-eye view.

His friend Ginger sat on the bottom step of the front stoop. She was only half attending to the conversation, the other half being occupied in giving her whiskers a thorough grooming.

Nubbin was stretched across the sidewalk at full cat length which, even without his missing tail, divided the walkway neatly in two, requiring passersby to ford him like a brook if they wanted to get from one side to the other.

A little out of the conversational loop as usual, Ratkin the rat was snugged down in the soft dirt between two roots of Pesky's tree where he could hear at will and doze at leisure.

"What is?" said Ginger, stroking a whisker.

"What is what?" asked Pesky.

"What do you mean, '*what is what*?'" said Ginger. "That's like asking a question about a question. Or putting one question inside another."

"Which is which?" said Ratkin. "Can't you be more specific?"

"I was asking Pesky what he used to say," said Ginger.

"What did he used to say?" said Nubbin, lifting his head from the sidewalk.

"Not Pesky but his old dad," said Ginger. "He was saying what he used to say."

"Wait a minute! Slow down! Who was saying what who used to say?" Nubbin looked confused.

"Me," said Pesky, "about my old dad. And Ginger was asking about what I said about my old dad."

"I've lost track of who was saying what about who to whom," said Ratkin.

"Me too," Pesky confessed, "I seem to have lost track of where I was going, and now I don't remember what it was I said my old dad used to say."

"Maybe we should start over," said Ginger. "Let's go back to the beginning. Pesky, why don't you say again what you said your dad said when you said to me what it was he used to say to you."

Pesky gave her a sidelong look.

"Are you trying to confuse me?"

"Yes," she admitted, and her mouth opened into a grin so wide it squeezed her golden eyes to slits.

"But only for fun," she went on. "You're always so serious, Pesky; it's hard not to tease you. Don't squirrels ever tease each other?"

"Sure they do," said Pesky. "Like my old dad used to tease me like I said just now."

"What exactly was it," said Ratkin, striking a blow for clarity, "that you said your old dad said to tease, Pesky?"

"Exactly what I said he said."

Ratkin sighed, "And what was that?"

"Let me think!" said Pesky, scratching his ear again. "Ah, now it's coming back to me. He said often—too often as a matter of fact—'Don't bury your acorns before they've fallen off the tree.'"

That was when Nubbin joined the conversation.

"That's the silliest thing I ever heard anybody say," he protested. "How can you bury acorns before they fall off the tree!"

"May I suggest," said Ratkin politely, "that that might have been the point? Actually, both their points. Or the same point of both. Pesky's dad was making use of the obvious, which is the last thing that most folks figure on. And Pesky was doing the same thing. Or trying to."

"Trying to what?" asked Nubbin.

"That's what I was asking him," said Ginger. "But now I think I get it. Pesky's dad was giving him advice but saying it like a joke. And so was Pesky when he said to me what his dad said to him."

She appealed for help.

"Was that what you meant, Pesky, when you said what you said about what your dad said?"

"That was what I meant to say," said Pesky.

"But," said Ginger, game to the last, "what did you mean when you said to me what he said to you? Cats don't bury acorns. We don't even like them."

"It sounds like a proverb," said Ratkin.

"What's a proverb?" asked Nubbin.

"A traditional saying," explained Ratkin. "The kind of thing someone says when they don't know what to say but want to say something. In this case, it sounds to me like Pesky meant the same thing his dad meant, which was 'Don't get in front of yourself by counting on something that hasn't happened yet.'"

"Why not?" said Ginger.

"Because it might not," said Ratkin.

"Might not what?" asked Ginger.

"What might not what?" said Nubbin, sitting upright with curiosity.

"Might not happen," said Ratkin.

"But what," said Ginger, "was it that I said that made Pesky say what he said about what I said?"

"Don't you remember?" said Pesky?

"Don't you?" said Ginger.

"Don't I what?" said Pesky.

"Remember!" prompted Ratkin, and muttered under his breath but still loud enough to be heard, "Am I the only one here who knows how to follow a straight line?"

"What's straight about it?" asked Nubbin, still curious. "We're talking about what Ginger said about what Pesky said his dad said. That's not a straight line, it's a zig-zag."

"It is not!" said Ratkin, adding under his breath but loud enough to be heard, "In fact it's a Gordian Knot."

"If it's a knot, it's not a line, and if it's either a knot or a line, it's not a zig-zag," said Ginger. "They can't all three be true at the same time."

"That's not what I meant to say at all," said Pesky, and scratched his other ear.

"That's a bunch of nonsense!" said Nubbin and put his head back down on the sidewalk.

"That's an unreliable balance," said Ginger, and she went back to her whiskers.

"That's philosophy," said Ratkin and went back to sleep.

The Tree and the Trash Can

Dusk was falling earlier every day, and autumn seemed just around the corner as the four friends gathered near the base of the tree, warming themselves with each other's conversation as well as their physical presence.

They were an odd mix a squirrel, two cats, and the rat who in the normal course of things should have been their victim but was instead their friend and mentor—but the combination suited them and harmed no one, and they were content with it and with each other.

"This is kind of like of when we lived in the trash can," mused Nubbin on one such evening. "Only different."

He was lying in his favorite spot, stretched full length across the sidewalk that skirted the tree, more than half asleep and letting his thoughts wander.

"What precisely do you mean by 'like but different?'" asked Ratkin. "I must confess I see very little in our situation that's like a trash can and a lot that's different."

Ratkin also was lying in his favorite spot, but his was the less exposed dirt hollow between two spreading roots of the tree. The softness of the dirt gave his skinny bones some comfort, and the roots were a bulwark between him and a world that by and large was not friendly to rats.

Nubbin licked a forepaw and gave his face a quick wash to wake himself up.

"I just meant that the trash can was a refuge for us cats in the big world that was the alley, and that's like what the tree is for us folks here now. Remember, Ginger?" he asked his sister.

"I guess I don't have the same memories you do," said Ginger. "This tree doesn't seem to me a bit like that trash can, or any trash can, for that matter. The trash can was dirty, noisy and dangerous. You've just forgotten."

She was sitting, as usual, on the bottom step of the front stoop across from the tree, her tail curled tidily around her paws.

Nubbin, who had no tail to curl, protested mildly. "No, I haven't forgotten," he said with a yawn. "I'm just not saying it very well. Ratkin could say it better."

"I'd say you're doing all right for the moment," said Ratkin. "Nothing lasts forever, though trees generally outlive trash cans."

As a rat, he faced a shorter life than either Pesky or the two cats, so he took a more thoughtful approach.

"All you can really say," he went on, "is that we're together for now, the four of us."

No one answered, so Nubbin went on, half to himself, half to Ginger.

"Remember when we lived in the trash can, that big grey cat with the tufty ears, Scuffer? How he used to lord it over us other cats? And fight with all the toms?"

"I remember him well," said Ginger, who had memories she did not share with Nubbin.

"But for all that," Nubbin went on, developing his notion, "he made us stay together in the trash can to be warm at night, even though we'd be having cat fights every day. I missed him when he died."

"How did he die?" asked Ratkin.

"Another cat, a stranger tom, challenged him to a fight. He lost."

"It happens."

"The King of the Trash Can," said Ginger as recollection darkened her eyes from green to lavender, "that was Scuffer. Do you know, Nubbin, he told me once he'd never been a pet? Never lived in a house, never lived with people. He was proud of being independent, always being on his own. That's what made him different from the rest of us strays and foundlings."

"What I remember is how much that difference mattered to him," said Nubbin. "How he boasted that he wasn't a <u>stray</u> cat; he was a <u>wild</u> cat and proud of it."

"He certainly acted like a wild cat the day he tangled with that tortoise-shell from the other end of the alley," Ginger chuckled, relishing the memory. "I'll never forget the yowl that came out of him as he swiped at its nose. It scared even me. And did that other fraidy-cat run!"

"It certainly frightened him," remembered Nubbin. "His howl was worse than his meow."

"Which was worse that his bite," said Ratkin, who never passed up an opportunity for an epigram if he could work one in, or even if he couldn't.

At that moment, the door of the house opened.

"Time for dinner," said Ginger. "Come on Nubbin." She trotted up the steps, followed by her brother.

"I'm hungry too," said Ratkin. "I'll have to find a dumpster to forage in."

The meeting broke up as the animals went their separate ways.

"See you tomorrow," waved Pesky.

But the next day brought them all an unpleasant surprise.

When Pesky emerged from the squirrel nest, he spotted Ratkin nestled in his usual place between the roots. But the rat wasn't snuggling comfortably, he was writhing and twisting in manifest pain.

"Hey Ratkin," Pesky called down, "are you alright?"

Ratkin heard, but could barely find the strength to answer. "Not exactly," he gasped with a gallant effort at his old humor. "Something I ate disagreed with me."

Pesky scrambled down the tree trunk but hesitated to approach.

"Sorry to be so trite," said the rat between gasps. "Poison in the dumpster." He convulsed, and his skinny body bent double with agony. He spoke no more.

Pesky was fixed in horror watching the dying rat when the house door opened and Ginger and Nubbin came out and down the steps. They saw at once that something was terribly wrong, and they clustered near Pesky but could find no way to help Ratkin.

All that day and into the night the animals stayed by Ratkin as much as they could, offering their presence in silent fellowship. The two cats refused to come in for dinner, and Pesky kept a silent vigil.

It was nearing morning when at last his writhing stopped and the rat lay still. Nubbin picked up a fallen leaf by the stem and carried it in his mouth to lay on Ratkin's limp body. One by one, Ginger and Pesky did the same.

"He was my best friend," said Nubbin by way of eulogy. He felt it was his place to pronounce, since he had known Ratkin longer than the others.

"I wouldn't be here right now if it weren't for Ratkin," he said. "I'd still be in the cage back in the Shelter. He brought me here, and it just isn't fair that I am here and he is gone. Things won't be the same without him."

"We won't be the same without him," said Pesky.

"We never were," said Ginger.

Mirabelle

It was a mild summer morning, and when Ginger woke him, Pesky the squirrel had been in the middle of his first nap of the day, dozing curled up in the crotch between two upspringing branches of the tree across from Ginger's house.

Ginger had climbed up to the level branch just below him, and was stretched full length along it, her tail hanging over the edge, where it twitched back and forth.

"I've been meaning to ask you..." she said.

"Ask away," Pesky murmured with a yawn.

He was used to Ginger's never-ending questions, though he was—perhaps fortunately—ignorant of the old adage that said curiosity had a way of killing cats.

"Okay," she said. "Here goes. Who is Mirabelle?"

"Oh, Mirabelle." Pesky looked uncomfortable.

"Yes, Mirabelle," said Ginger.

The way Pesky said the name told her at once that she had stumbled on to something significant, though she didn't yet know what that something was, or why or how it was important.

"I asked you who she was once before," she reminded him. "Remember? When you were talking in your sleep and said her name. And you just mumbled , 'Someone I know,' so I figured she must have been part of a dream. But if you had a dream about Mirabelle, she must have been important. And if she was important to you, I should know about her, because I'm your best friend. After all, I told you all about Nubbin, how he's my lost and found brother and all that."

"You did indeed," admitted Pesky. "So I guess you deserve to know about my lost and <u>not</u> found Mirabelle. Ah, Mirabelle." His eyes took on a faraway look that Ginger had never seen before. "I only saw her once," he confessed. "But she wasn't a dream. Not then, anyway."

A sigh escaped him, and his whiskers twitched as memory swept him back.

"She was a beautiful red squirrel with tufted ears, a furry white tummy and a feathery tail. The first time I saw her—the only time I saw her—she and another squirrel, a grey squirrel named Ruffo, were chasing each other up and down and around and around the tree next over from mine, where we are right now. But she was smaller than

Ruffo, and faster than he was, and she was getting ahead of him, and he called out, 'Hold up Mirabelle! Wait for me!'

"That's how I learned her name.

"But she wasn't about to stop and wait for him. Not my Mirabelle! She just called back, 'Catch me if you can!' and at the same time she took a flying leap from the tip end of one branch to the tip end of one on the next tree over, which was mine. She looked like a bird, a beautiful bird with legs instead of wings, and a plumey tail for balance."

Pesky's eyes sparkled with recollection.

"The branch where she landed bent nearly double under her weight, but she kept on running, straight up the length of the branch and straight down the tree and on to the next tree, which was mine. She was laughing fit to bust, and as she passed me she gave a little wink that said I was in on the joke. Her laughter made that other squirrel *so* mad he had sparks coming out of his ears.

"She was the prettiest thing I ever saw," Pesky went on, deep in his memories "Though I never saw her but that once."

"What, never?" asked Ginger. "All that memory and you only saw her once?"

"In my mind's eye I see her all the time," he mused. "There are some things, Ginger," he continued, and his words were heavy with recollection, "that are forever."

"I guess you're talking about love at first sight," said Ginger.

An unexpected image of Scuffer, the big grey fighting tom from her early days in the trash can, came prowling uninvited into her mind, bringing with him stray memories of her younger self.

"What I'm talking about,' said Pesky, "are once-in-a-lifetime events. If you are lucky enough to have such an event happen to you, you never forget the experience."

Ginger felt a need to change the subject.

"You're starting to sound just like Ratkin," she said.

"Am I? How did Ratkin sound?" asked Pesky.

"Preachy and tiresome," said Ginger.

"Ratkin had a lot to say because he knew a lot about a lot of things," said Pesky. "I'm sorry he's gone. I miss him."

"I miss him too," she confessed. "In spite of his everlastingly having the answers to everything. I think it's sad the way friends come and go. I wish the world would stay put."

"Now it's you who's starting to sound like Ratkin," said Pesky. "When you say you want the world to 'stay put,' what you really mean is you want it to stay put where you left it. If the world had 'stayed put' before you came here, you'd never even have known Ratkin."

"And," he added, "you and I would never have gotten to know each other either. You'd never have come face to face with that awful dog, or escaped up my tree, or...or anything," he finished lamely.

Do cats laugh? Ginger did.

That is to say, her whiskers quivered, and her golden eyes narrowed to slits, and the tip of her tail started a little a dance of its own independent of the rest of its length.

"Why Pesky," she said with mock seriousness, "you really are a preacher. I think you've missed your calling."

Pesky did not thank her for the compliment.

"Blast it!" he muttered. "I'm starting to sound just like my old dad. And I swore to myself years ago that I would never ever allow that to happen."

"Who's being silly now?" teased Ginger. "I kind of like your old dad. At least," she added, "what I remember about him from what you tell me you remember about him."

The laughter in her eyes brought an end to the argument. Pesky made rather a point of going back to his nap, snuggling down into the leaves and squeezing shut his eyes, while Ginger gave her face a thorough wash and carefully smoothed her whiskers and curled her tail neatly around her front paws.

But they both understood without either saying it that the conversation, though it had come to a halt, was far from over, and could be carried on at another time.

And in another story.

Old Dad

I t was one of those late summer days when the warm breeze carries an under-tang of autumn and the leaves are starting to fall too early in the season, before their edges have crisped or their hue has lost its green.

On this lovely, bittersweet day two curiously matched yet ill-assorted friends, Ginger the house-cat and Pesky the tree-squirrel, were chatting together in the maple tree.

Ginger was stretched full length along her usual branch, the sturdy one that jutted at right-angles from the trunk, her tail with its slight curl at the tip hanging down behind her.

Pesky was perched facing her at the farther end of the same branch.

He was holding a maple seed-pod between his paws, nibbling at it and letting the crumbs fall wherever they would.

"Tell me some more about your dad," said Ginger. "I like hearing your stories about him."

At her question, his face shut like a trap in a look she had never seen before.

"What more do you want to know?" he asked her between nibbles.

"Whatever else there is to know," she said.

Pesky kept silent, so she went on.

"He comes up in conversation a lot. I hear you talk about '*my old dad*' this and '*my old dad*' that, but you never say enough about him for me to feel like I know the person you're talking about."

"He was something, my old dad." Pesky tilted his head to one side and closed his eyes in remembrance. "A real character, sure enough."

"Did the 'real character' have a real name?"

"Everyone called him Ranter," said Pesky, "from how he was always chattering and carrying on."

"*Ranter*," said Ginger, testing it on her tongue. "That doesn't sound at all like a proper name for a squirrel."

"It wasn't; it was just what folks called him, because he'd get into a conversation with anyone who came his way but it always wound up with him doing most of the talking. The name fit him, though,' said Pesky, "like it was made for him. Come to think of it, it was made for him."

He added, "He'd have loved you, Ginger, because you're always asking questions."

"I am now," said Ginger, "but I wasn't always. We didn't have dads in the trash can, so there was no one to ask back then."

"He had a story or a proverb for every occasion," said Pesky with a reminiscent smile. "The kits in the Nest loved my dad because he used to tell them stories. If it was raining, say, or too wet to play outside, the little ones used to snuggle down into the leaves in the Nest and listen to him by the hour."

"Go on," said Ginger. "That's the kind of thing I want to hear about."

Pesky went on. "There was one little kit who was his special pet. He called her Yakki because she never shut up. They were two of a kind, my old dad and Yakki. Like calling to like, I always thought. I remember one day..."

His voice trailed off.

"What," asked Ginger "do you remember? That's just the kind of thing I want to hear."

"No you don't," said Pesky.

"Yes I do," said Ginger.

"Well then, I don't want to say. Okay?"

"But why not? What happened?"

"A bad thing."

"Go on," said Ginger.

Pesky sighed.

"My dad was telling her a story about the adventures of a baby squirrel named Yakki. The real Yakki was so small she almost fell off the branch, but he held her spellbound."

He stopped again.

"Go on, go on," said Ginger.

"Well, there they were, just having a good time, and this boy came along..."

Again he stopped.

"What boy?" asked Ginger.

"Nobody special," said Pesky. "Just a boy playing on the sidewalk underneath the tree. Not a big kid, but old enough to play by himself. He was..."

Pesky stopped, and Ginger waited patiently till he made himself go on.

"He was throwing stones. Just for fun it looked to me like, trying if he could throw well enough to hit anything—knots in tree-trunks or cracks in the sidewalk, it didn't seem to matter. Well, he heard my dad and Yakki chattering at each other. He looked up and saw them sitting on a branch just over his head, and..."

"And?" asked Ginger. "What happened then?"

"He had a stone in his hand all ready to throw. So he threw it at the two of them."

A quiver went through Pesky from whiskers to tail-end as he tried to shake off the memory.

"It missed Yakki by a hair and scared her half to death, but it hit my dad bang on the side of his head so hard it knocked him off the branch. A lucky throw; nobody could aim that well."

Pesky took a breath, then went on.

"I saw him fall. He fell so slowly. Sometimes even now, when I shut my eyes I can see him falling falling. He landed—thud! just like that—in the dirt at the foot of the tree right in front of the boy. He lay so still I knew right away he was dead. Just another dead leaf to lead the way for autumn."

The pause that followed lasted so long Ginger became afraid to break it.

She finally asked, "What did the boy do?"

"He didn't do anything," said Pesky. "He just walked away."

"But that's terrible!" said Ginger. "How could he leave your dad lying in the dirt?"

Her tail twitched and she closed her eyes to shut out the vision. "I wish you hadn't told me," she said.

"I tried not to," said Pesky.

For a while they both were silent, together yet apart, each with separate thoughts.

At last Ginger spoke.

"Where were you?" she asked.

"Too close," was all Pesky said.

There seemed nothing more to add.

"But why?" she asked. "That's what I don't understand. Why did the boy throw the stone?"

"I don't know," said Pesky. He shrugged. "Because he could, I guess."

Life After Life

"How is Yakki?" Nubbin asked Pesky, "I haven't seen her for a while."

Nubbin was curled next to his sister Ginger on the front stoop of the house across from the maple tree.

Both cats were industriously washing their faces and whiskers, the regular after-breakfast grooming that officially launched them on the rest of their day.

Nubbin's question had an air of a casual enquiry that was at odds with his genuine concern for its subject.

The Yakki he asked about had as a young squirrel been chatting with Pesky the squirrel's old dad when a boy threw a stone that knocked him unconscious, and he fell off his perch. As a witness to his death, Yakki had taken it hard and was apparently still dealing with the after-effects.

From his usual perch on his favorite branch of the maple tree, Pesky had a squirrel's-eye view of the stoop and his two cat friends.

"Yakki?" he answered. "Oh, she's all right."

He fell silent, then heaved a great sigh.

"Well, actually no, not so good."

Nobody answered, so he elaborated.

"She doesn't seem to want to come out and chase around with the other squirrels like she used to. My guess is that what happened to my dad that day upset her, sitting right there next to him as she was when he was killed."

"It would certainly have upset me," said Nubbin, "and I'm not even a squirrel."

"It's been a while since it happened," said Pesky sadly, "but it still haunts her. She keeps on asking me where my old dad is now. As if he just went out looking for acorns and would be coming back."

"That's just the way it was in the Shelter," said Nubbin. "Remember, Ginger? How in the Shelter animals would just disappear from time to time and we never knew where they had gone to? One day somebody'd be scuffling to get at the food bowls like the rest of us, and the next day—gone—poof—just like that!"

"Someone always came," Ginger reminded him, "and took them away. When we were sleeping, mostly. So we didn't see."

"Like the Great Squirrel," said Pesky.

"Who's the Great Squirrel?" asked Nubbin. "I never heard of him."

"No," said Pesky. "You're a cat. He wouldn't be in your stories. But all us squirrels know about the Great Squirrel."

"Tell me about him," said Nubbin.

Pesky took a big breath and let it out.

"The Great Squirrel," he said, "is so big that you can't see him. He is so big he fills up all the spaces in between things. He is everywhere. He can blow the leaves off the trees just by breathing, and when he closes his eyes the whole word goes dark. His fur is made of un-mown grass; his eyes have the light of brown pebbles under sunlit water; and his tail is tufted with bramble bushes."

Nubbin shut his eyes and kept them shut. Then he opened them wide and shook his head.

"I tried," he said, "but I can't get my eyes around anything that big."

"That's the whole point," said Pesky. "That's exactly what I've just been telling you. He's too big to fit into your eyes. He's bigger than we can see. Or say."

"That's pretty big," agreed Nubbin.

"Big enough to carry us all to the Topmost Nest when our time comes," said Pesky proudly.

"What's the Topmost Nest?" asked Nubbin, as curious as the cat in the adage.

Pesky waved his paw in a vague circle. "It's the place where we all go when our time comes," he said.

"But where is that?" asked Nubbin.

Again Pesky waved his paw. "Somewhere way up above the treetops. The Great Squirrel comes for us all sooner or later. Oftentimes he comes when you're asleep. Kind of sneaks up on you. It's a good thing he does, too. Otherwise..."

Pesky twitched his whiskers, and his mouth stretched in what looked very much like a smile.

Ginger pounced on that. "What are you grinning about?" she asked him.

He shrugged.

"I'm just thinking what a crowded Nest we'd be living in if all the squirrels who've ever lived were still around. If it weren't for the Great Squirrel, they'd all still be here, and what a mob that would make! The Great Squirrel keeps the world from filling up with too many squirrels. Isn't there anything like that for cats?"

"I don't think cats have a Topmost Nest," said Nubbin. "I've never heard of such a thing. Have you, Ginger?"

"There was something they used to tell in the Shelter," said Ginger, "about the Forever Cage where the cats went when they disappeared."

"I don't remember that," said Nubbin. "What was it?"

"Well," said Ginger, "the way it went, the Forever Cage was a wonderful place where the food bowls were always full and the fights always ended with everybody back where they started."

The others were listening, big-eyed, so she went on.

"The Forever Cage was so much bigger than the regular cage that when you were inside it, you couldn't even see the edges. Like it was everywhere."

"I get it!" said Nubbin. "Like it goes on forever. Right?"

"Right," said Ginger.

"Go on," said Pesky. "This is getting interesting."

Ginger flexed her front claws to give her time to think. She took a deep breath and continued.

"The Forever Cage is so big it fills up all the spaces between things. Its walls are made of woven air, and the big gate opens into an even bigger room called Outside where no one ever gets to go."

"I see," said Pesky, and he added, "That's not exactly the same as a Topmost Nest, but it certainly sounds better than the cage in the Shelter."

"It's a good thing to think about," said Ginger, "but to me it sounds too good to be true."

No one had an answer to that, so she went on.

"But maybe that's what stories are meant to do, to give you something to think about that will take your mind off..."

She squeezed her eyes shut in concentration.

"...off all the things you think about when you're thinking about things you don't want to think about."

She paused, then added, "If you know what I mean."

"I know what you mean," said Pesky.

"Me, too," said Nubbin.

Like Ginger, he flexed his claws. Like Ginger, it gave him time to think.

He was silent for a moment; then he came out with it, "Maybe someone ought to try telling Yakki a story, like Pesky's old dad was doing when he died."

Everybody thought that was a fine idea. For somebody else.

The silence grew.

And grew.

"I guess it's up to me," said Pesky finally. "So I will."

So he did.

A Bedtime Story

It was a warm summer evening, filled with the glow of a late-setting sun, and the squirrels were making the most of the light by chasing each other round and round and round the trunk of the maple tree.

When the sun was gone and bedtime approaching, the tired-out squirrel kits retired to the Nest perched in the highest crook of the topmost branches of the maple tree, where they snuggled deep in the dried leaves and promptly fell asleep.

Except for the kit they called Yakki, who would always rather talk than sleep. Yakki usually tried to fight off sleep, first by not snuggling down and second by chattering nonstop to the squirrel she called "Uncle," whose other name was Pesky.

On this particular evening Pesky was perched precariously upon a slender branch just above the Nest that swayed up and down and back and forth as the wind blew it about.

From this shifting vantage-point, he could see that Yakki was yawning hugely and rubbing her eyes with both paws.

"Looks like bedtime," he suggested.

"Not for me," said Yakki, and she swallowed a yawn so he wouldn't notice.

"I'm not a bit sleepy. And Granddad always said bedtime was the best time for story-telling. I'm so sad and sorry that he's gone. So tell a story, please Uncle Pesky, like Granddad used to do."

Then she curled herself into a furry ball, tucked her tail under her chin, and wriggled herself a place in the leaves.

"Okay, I'm all ready," she announced.

"So I see," said Pesky. He took a deep breath, tilted his head on one side, and began.

"Once upon a time..."

He got no further before Yakki broke in, as she almost always did. Pesky sighed. He was fond of Yakki, but he couldn't help wishing that once in a while, just once in a while, she would let him tell a story without interrupting. This time she asked, "What does that mean?"

"What does what mean?"

"What you just said—'once upon a time.'"

Pesky blinked in confusion, so she went on to explain.

"You always start your stories like that, and I keep meaning to ask you about it, and then I get stuck in the story and forget to ask. But now I remember what I forgot. *Up on* means 'on top of,' doesn't it? Like *up on* a tree or *up on* a branch? But how can you be *up on* a time?"

In need of inspiration, Pesky stretched his left hind paw forward to scratch his left ear, the one he always reached for when he was in need of inspiration.

There was a pause while he gave his ear a good scratch. Then, "You can't," he finally admitted. "Not really."

Yakki said nothing, and he felt that something more was needed.

"But 'upon a time' doesn't actually mean 'on top of.' It's just a fancy way of saying 'long ago,' or 'in olden times,' so folks listening to the story will know it isn't nowadays."

There was a pause while Yakki took her time to think about that.

To help her thinking, she uncurled her tail, rubbed her nose with her front paw, scratched an ear with her hind paw, and twitched her whiskers. When she had done with all these activities and not a minute before, only then did she declare:

"That's an awful lot of trouble to go to. Why not just say 'long ago' or 'in olden times' to start with?"

"Because..." Pesky's scratching paw got busier to give him time to think. When his paw had done its job, he continued.

"...because if I said 'long ago' you might think it was real and not made up. A story is a tale about what happened; it's not the happening itself."

It started to come easier as he warmed to his subject.

"I mean, if it was real, it wouldn't be a story, now would it?"

"Because," he went on, "here you are all tucked up in the tree ready for sleep, but when you hear me say *once upon a time*, that tells you to get ready for a special time. A story time."

Yakki bounced so energetically that leaves went flying in all directions, and Yakki herself almost fell out of the Nest.

"I get it!" she said and clasped her paws with excitement. "Thank you, Uncle Pesky, I really get it! I see now what *upon a time* means to mean. Start the story over again, and this time I won't interrupt, I promise!"

"Promise?"

"Promise! Cross my heart and hope to die. Stick a pine cone in my eye!"

"Well, then, okay. Once upon a time," said Pesky very slowly, very carefully, "there was a squirrel who wanted to be an acorn."

He paused for a half-breath, waiting for her to say how silly that was, but Yakki nodded her head in silent agreement, as if giving him her permission to go on.

So he did.

"Now you may think," he said, "that was the wrong way round and that it would be more fitting for an acorn to want to be a squirrel. Not so, but far otherwise."

"Especially not for this particular squirrel, whose name was Bertie. Bertie gazed with envy on the smooth brown skin of the acorn and with admiration at the cap on its head that kept the sunshine off and looked so stylish.

"'How handsome you look!' he said to the acorn one day.

'Me? Handsome?' said Ilex (for Ilex was the acorn's name). 'Get away! I look just like all the other acorns.'

'That's exactly my point,' said Bertie. 'You don't look like a squirrel. I'd like to have a cap like yours. It looks so jaunty, as if whoever wore it would have a good time.'"

"That's a funny word, *jaunty*," said Yakki to Pesky.

Then she said it again to savor the taste of the sound. "Jaunty."

She rolled it around the inside of her mouth. " Jauuunty."

Then she shouted at the top of her lungs. "JAUNTYYY!!!"

"Not so loud!" said Pesky, trying in vain to hush her. "You'll wake the other kits."

"The other kits are not asleep," said Yakki. "They're listening to every single word we say."

'"We are so too asleep!" said a squirrely voice from deep down under the leaves. "So SHUT UP!"

Pesky twitched his whiskers.

Yakki closed her eyes...

...and Pesky continued telling the story, but in a softer voice so as not to waken the sleeping kits, and the story went on until it came to its end.

And there it stopped.

And Yakki?

She fell fast asleep in spite of herself and dreamed about a squirrel who wore an acorn cap and an acorn that wore a squirrel cap.

The acorn's name was Jaunty. The squirrel's name was Yakki.

Pesky's Dream

P esky the squirrel was having an adventure. Snuggled deep in his treetop nest piled with last year's leaves, he was deep in a dream in which he was both the chief participant and the all-important audience.

All the action was at once speeded up and slowed down, as if he were watching it happen to someone else.

For Pesky to dream was not in itself unusual. He spent a lot of his time dreaming, and enjoyed his dreams as a pastime. He had a lively interior life that often carried him over from waking into sleep and back again, and oftentimes he found it difficult to distinguish one state from the other.

But this dream was unlike his ordinary sleep-history, for though it happened <u>to</u> him, it was not <u>about</u> him, no, no not at all.

As Pesky watched, it dawned on him that he was not in his tree, but in a round and rickety space that he knew without knowing was a trash can tipped on its side. It was a space where he had never been, and yet he recognized it right away as the cramped and bangy trash can in which his friend Ginger the cat had grown up. He was seeing it through her eyes, though it never occurred to Pesky to wonder how or why, as the scene before his eyes took all his attention.

Two cats balanced unsteadily on the rolling floor of the can. They were were engaged in a face-off. Ears were flattened, tails were lashing, and the air vibrated with hisses, yowls and low growls that were at the same time ominous and utterly silent, as if watched through a window. One of the cats was a brindled grey with darker stripes. The other was a tortoise-shell, a mix of red and black, raggedy and patched where the fur had been scarred or torn.

The grey cat was the big tom with the tufty ears Ginger had talked about. The tortoise-shell was a stranger. Both were uncomfortably close to Pesky. He could see in clear detail the stiffened upright hairs along each cat's backbone, see their bared teeth as each cat screeched a challenge at the other. The atmosphere was charged with tension. Pesky knew that something bad was about to happen, and he found it difficult to breathe. He listened hard, for though there was a lot of noise, there was at the same time no sound.

That being the case, it must be counted as odd that he heard every word of their silent conversation.

"Stand and fight!" snarled the tortoise-shell cat, tossing a challenge at the grey. "I can beat you any day, and today I will!"

"Yah, well we'll see about that, tough guy," sneered the grey in equal silence. "You're nothing but a bully!'

"I'm tougher than you, you coward!"

"You're the coward!

"Scaredy-cat!"

"Butter-paws!"

"Mouse-turd!"

"Sissy!"

"Wimp!"

"Wuss!"

Tiring at last of hurling insults, the two cats began instead to stalk stiff-legged around and around each other, circling while keeping a safe distance between them.

Then they reversed the circle for a couple more rounds. Then they stood stock-still, and for an endless moment time paused and the world inside the trash can held its breath.

And then, in the slow-motion action of dreams he saw each cat take a murderous swipe at his opposite number, claws extended, gleaming and sharp as knives.

Neither of the swipes connected with either cat, and the Pesky who was Ginger understood that they were a feint, the opening moves in a ritual procedure where the rules and guidelines were understood on both sides.

Then as if at a signal both cats lunged at one another, rolling with the trash can as it rolled, scratching and screeching and clawing with jungle ferocity like some strange combined animal with multiple limbs engaged in a fight to the death with itself.

The dreaming Pesky looked on with close attention as this hybrid creature, without making a sound, unwound itself and broke back into two that circled, spitting before lunging at itself again and rolling some more.

How long this went on he had no notion, only that it seemed eternal yet immediate, action perpetually in motion but perpetually unresolved.

Part of him took time out to marvel at the complexity of dreams.

I guess it all depends, he finally decided, *on who is watching*.

And then he wondered if it was really Ginger and not him, or if he and Ginger were the same sort of combined creature as the rolling, fighting hybrid beast.

He amused himself briefly by wondering how the two cats would look at him and Ginger if they could see them and if their roles were reversed.

But they did not know he was dreaming them. Or did they?

But am I really dreaming them? he wondered. *Or are they dreaming me? Or are we all dreaming each other?*

The questions were too much for even Pesky's insatiable curiosity, and he was glad to discard them.

Instead, he became aware that there were others in the trash can besides himself and the two fighters. These others—whether squirrels or cats he could not tell—crowded into the edges of his vision like standing-room-only spectators at a show, their ghostly heads bobbing and ducking as they followed the fight.

Maybe they have nothing else to do, speculated Pesky. *I guess it's one way to spend your time.*

The prospect of such an everlasting dream fight, one that just went on and on, was so exhausting that it made his head hurt, so he decided to wake up.

But though he tried as hard as his dreaming mind could manage, he wasn't able to do that either. He would think he was awake and that his eyes were open, and then realize that no, they were still closed and he was still stuck in the dream, caught in a loop that kept him coming back again and again to the same cats in the same fight.

For as everyone knows, a dream is not like a story that has a beginning, a middle, and an end. Dreams have no "once upon a time," let alone any "happy ever after." Dreams start in the middle, and they do not come to a conclusion, satisfying or otherwise. On the contrary, they go on going on until such time as the dreamer wakes up or changes to another dream.

And perhaps it is there that we should leave them all—in that silent, unreal actuality and imagination, between the regular everyday world and the much more mysterious other one that haunts our sleep.

Or it is we who haunt it in our sleep?

Whichever may be the case, perhaps it is time to say goodbye to it, and to the two fighting cats and the trash can filled with memories, and most of all, goodbye to the dreaming Pesky who is trying so hard to wake up.

That is, until the next time he and his motley crew of phantasms decide they are in the mood for another story.

Or another dream.

A Trash Can Full of Memories

When they were kittens, Ginger and Nubbin—though he wasn't called Nubbin then because he still had his tail—lived with other cats in the overturned trash can in the alley. Their hero was Scuffer, the big grey fighting tom with the tufty ears who lorded it over the trash can.

Ginger developed a terrific crush on Scuffer, and adored him from afar. She dreamed about him and followed his every move with worshipful attention.

Nubbin, known then as Runtie because he was the runt of his litter, also dreamed about Scuffer, but for a different reason. Nubbin wanted to be Scuffer when he grew up and tried to give himself a head start by practicing growls in his sleep.

But time went on and circumstances changed. Ginger and Nubbin grew from kittens to cats, and left the trash can for the animal Shelter. It was there that Nubbin lost his tail and got his nickname, and it was there that Nubbin found a rodent friend named Ratkin, but he does not come into this story. After that they lived in the house near the tree where Pesky the squirrel had his nest, and the three of them became good friends.

It got to be a custom that on long summer evenings the two cats would regale Pesky with the stories they remembered about life in the trash can. This was partly to entertain him and partly to keep their memories alive in a confusing and distracting world. As they spun their yarns, the battered, rusty refuse pail became a kind of outdoor library filled with folktales and sagas and epics and romances, with stories of adventure and suspense.

Here is a story Ginger told one summer evening, with help from Nubbin.

"It was late afternoon in the trash can," she said, "and we were all asleep, napping before our regular prowl up and down the alley in search of dinner.

"I was dozing near the open end of the can, and Nubbin was curled next to me..."

"I wasn't asleep," said Nubbin. "I was on guard like Scuffer."

"...when a shadow fell across us both," continued Ginger. "I looked up and there standing in the open space was the scruffiest-looking-looking tomcat you ever saw, a tortoise-shell mix of red and black. His fur was ragged, torn and scarred from what looked like a lifetime's worth of fights with other cats.

"I was starting to back away when I heard a growl behind me. It was Scuffer, awake and on guard."

"Just like me," said Nubbin. "So Scuffer growled, 'Get away from those kittens!' and the tortoise-shell snarled back 'Try and make me!'

"And Scuffer hissed, 'Okay, mister tough guy!'

"And the tortoise-shell hissed back, 'I'm tougher than you are, you coward!'

"And Scuffer told him, 'You're the coward!'

"The tortoise-shell said, 'Fraidy-cat!'

"Scuffer said, 'Butter-paws!'

"The tortoise-shell said, 'Mouse-turd!'

"Scuffer said, 'Sissy!'

"'Wimp!'

"'Wuss!'"

Seeing that Nubbin was getting off track, Ginger took over the narrative.

"They began to stalk around and around each other, very stern and stiff-legged, all the while making sure there was a safe distance between them. Then they reversed and went the other way for several more rounds.

"Then they stood staring at each other for what seemed like an age.

"Then each cat took a swipe at the other, but neither of the swipes hit home.

"They weren't meant to. They were just the opening moves, mere gestures, feints in a pattern of battle.

"Then as if at a signal, both cats lunged at the same time, and the trash can rocked back and forth, and the cats screeched and scratched and clutched at each other. They looked for all the world like some hybrid animal with too many legs having a fight with itself.

"And then the hybrid split back into two cats that circled spitting at one another before lunging back into itself again and rolling around some more.

"The other cats in the trash can crowded around, all eager to see, their heads bobbing up and down as they followed the fight."

"What happened then?" asked Pesky.

"Oh," said Ginger, yawning, "we watched them fight for a while, and then Scuffer chased the tortoise-shell out of the trash can and all the way down the alley. When he came back to make sure me and Nubbin were okay, he had a torn ear, and the two of us took turns licking it to help it heal."

"And then what?" asked Pesky.

"Then we all went out for dinner," said Ginger, "to celebrate his victory."

"That's quite a story," said Pesky. "Have you told it before?"

"Once or twice," said Ginger. "Mostly to remind Nubbin. He tends to forget details."

"Did the tortoise-shell ever come back?" asked Pesky. "Afterwards, I mean."

"No way!" said Ginger. "He was well and truly scared out of his skin. Scuffer roughed him up so bad he had to go looking for another alley."

She smiled with satisfaction.

"He was some cat, that Scuffer. The King of the Trash Can. Tough, but gentle. He was so kind to me when I was just a kit. I don't think I'll ever forget him."

Her eyes looked inward, scanning memories.

"I know just how you feel," said Pesky, and Ginger knew he was thinking about Mirabelle.

"There are some things," he went on reminiscently, "that are forever. Once-in-a-lifetime events."

"You've said that before," said Ginger.

"And it's worth saying again," said Pesky. "If you are fortunate enough to have someone that important in your life, you should never forget them."

"Then I guess I'm fortunate," said Ginger, "to have a trash can full of memories."

"That's a lot of memories," mused Pesky. "Enough to last a lifetime."

"A cat lifetime," added Ginger with feline pride. "And that adds up to nine ordinary ones."